W9-BLT-553

The Lion and the Mouse

Adapted by Sarah Toast
Illustrated by Krista Brauckmann-Towns
Other illustrations by Marty Noble

7373 North Cicero Avenue, Lincolnwood, Illinois 60712
Ground Floor, 59 Gloucester Place, London W1U 8JJ
Customer Service: 1-800-595-8484 or customer_service@pilbooks.com
www.pilbooks.com
Permission is never granted for commercial purposes.
p i kids is a registered trademark of Publications International, Ltd.
8 7 6 5 4 3 2 1
ISBN-13: 978-1-4127-8268-5
ISBN-10: 1-4127-8268-6

 publications international, ltd.

Once there was a happy little gray mouse. The mouse loved to scamper, and hide, and squeak, and all sorts of other mouse things. But most of all, this little mouse loved to eat. She didn't love to eat just anything, either. The mouse especially loved to eat plump, juicy berries.

All summer long, the mouse scurried about, feasting on the plentiful ripe berries that had dropped from the vine. But as the months passed, berries were harder to find lying around on the ground. The mouse had to look harder every day just to find her favorite food.

One day a lion was taking a nice nap in the sun. Nearby, the busy little mouse scurried about looking for berries, but all the berries that were left were too high to reach. Then the mouse spotted a lovely bunch of berries that she could reach by climbing the rock below them. When she did, the mouse discovered that she hadn't climbed a rock at all. She had climbed right on top of the lion's head!

The lion did not like to be bothered while he was sleeping. He awoke with a loud grumble. "Who dares to tickle my head while I'm taking a nap?" he roared.

The little mouse scrambled to get away from the lion, but he was too quick. The lion scooped the mouse up in his paw.

"Little mouse," roared the lion. "Don't you know that I am the king of the forest? Why did you wake me up from my pleasant nap by tickling my head?"

"Oh please, lion," said the mouse. "I was only trying to get some lovely berries."

"Just see how much you like it when I tickle your head," said the lion.

"Please, lion," pleaded the mouse. "If you spare me, I am sure I will be able to help you someday."

Suddenly the lion began to smile. Then he began to snicker. Then he began to chuckle. Soon he was roaring with laughter! He laughed so hard his tummy began to ache, and a little tear trickled out of his eye.

"How could you, a tiny mouse, help the most powerful animal in the forest?" said the lion, still sputtering with laughter. "That's so funny, I'll let you go — this time."

Then the lion laughed some more. He rolled over on his back, kicking in a fit of giggles. The mouse had to leap out of his way to avoid being crushed. Off she ran, as fast as she could.

Still chuckling, the lion got up and set out to find some lunch. It wasn't long before he smelled food. Walking toward the good smell, the lion suddenly found himself caught in a trap that had recently been set by hunters.

The lion was stuck in the strong ropes, and the more he struggled, the tighter they held him. Fearing the hunters would soon return, the terrified lion roared for help.

The mouse heard the lion's roars from far away. At first she was afraid to go back, thinking the lion might hurt her. But the lion's cries for help made the mouse sad.

The mouse also remembered her promise to help the lion. She hurried to where he was tangled in the trap.

"Oh lion," said the mouse. "I know what it feels like to be caught. But don't worry. I'll try to help you."

"There's nothing you can do," said the lion. "These ropes are very strong."

Suddenly the mouse said, "I have an idea!" She quickly began chewing through the thick ropes with her small, sharp teeth. She worked and worked, and before long, the mouse had chewed through enough rope for the lion to get out of the trap!

The lion was very grateful to the mouse. "Thank you for saving me," he said. "I am sorry that I laughed at you before."

Then the lion scooped up the mouse and placed her on his head. He carried her back to the berry bush and lay down under it. "Mouse," he said, "reach up and pick one of those berries."

The mouse plucked the very biggest berry. The lion took the mouse in his paw and said, "Let's stick together. I can help you reach the berries, and you can get me out of a tight spot now and then."

And they've been friends ever since.

Friendship

Friendship is wonderful. The more people you share it with, the better it is. In this story, the lion and the mouse learned how fun it is to make new friends.

At first the lion and mouse did not want to be friends. But in the end they discovered that even though they are very different, they can still be good friends.